Boys are nothing but trouble!

"Mooseboy *can't* come to Sweet Valley Elementary!" Jessica whined. "He's a *boy*."

I shook my head. "Boys can be fun. Todd is."

"But Todd's not a furry, frozen, raw-fish-eating boy!" Jessica snapped.

"Oooh, Jessica's *boy*friend's coming to see her," Charlie teased.

Some of the other boys joined in. "Jessica's got a *boy*friend! Jessica's got a *boy*friend!"

Jessica covered her red cheeks with her hands. "See what I mean? Boys are *dumb!*"

Bantam Books in the SWEET VALLEY KIDS series

SWEET VALLEY BLIZZARD!

Written by
Molly Mia Stewart

Created by
FRANCINE PASCAL

Illustrated by
Marcy Ramsey

BANTAM BOOKS
NEW YORK • TORONTO • LONDON • SYDNEY • AUCKLAND

RL 2, 005-008

SWEET VALLEY BLIZZARD!
A Bantam Book / January 1998

*Sweet Valley High® and Sweet Valley Kids® are
registered trademarks of Francine Pascal.*

Conceived by Francine Pascal.

*Produced by Daniel Weiss Associates, Inc.
33 West 17th Street
New York, NY 10011.*

Cover art by Wayne Alfano.

ISBN: 0-553-48343-9

Published simultaneously in the United States and Canada

Bantam Books are published by Bantam Books, a division of Bantam
Doubleday Dell Publishing Group, Inc. Its trademark, consisting of the
words "Bantam Books" and the portrayal of a rooster, is Registered in the
U.S. Patent and Trademark Office and in other countries. Marca
Registrada. Bantam Books, 1540 Broadway, New York, New York 10036.

PRINTED IN THE UNITED STATES OF AMERICA

OPM   0 9 8 7 6 5 4 3 2 1

To Bailey Silverman

CHAPTER 1

A Letter from Mooseboy

"We've got a lot of mail today," our teacher, Mr. Crane, announced. His mailbag was filled with letters. "And it's all from your Alaskan pen pals!"

Everyone cheered and clapped. Everyone but Jessica Wakefield, my twin sister.

"I hope Kiki sent me a picture of her family like she promised," Amy Sutton said. She turned to me. "How about your pen pal, Elizabeth?"

"Sally sent me a cool rock last time," I replied.

Jessica rolled her eyes. "I hope Mooseboy didn't send me *anything*. He'd probably send me bear claws or something gross like that."

"His name isn't Mooseboy," I reminded her. "It's Bob Burdett. Don't be goofy."

I guess I should introduce myself. I'm Elizabeth Wakefield. Jessica and I are identical twins. We both have long blond hair with bangs and blue-green eyes. And we have a dimple in our left cheek when we smile. We look so much alike that people get us mixed up.

We're second graders in Mr. Crane's class at Sweet Valley Elementary. At school we wear name bracelets so everyone can tell us apart. I like to wear my hair in a ponytail, but Jessica wears hers down. When we want to fool people, we both wear our hair the

2

same way. It drives everyone crazy. Especially our big brother, Steven.

My favorite sport is soccer, and I like riding horses too. Jessica thinks soccer is too rough and that horses smell. She likes to play princess and dress-up instead. My best friends, besides Jessica of course, are Todd Wilkins and Amy. Jessica's best friends, besides me, are Ellen Riteman and Lila Fowler.

I love school, especially reading. Homework doesn't bug me. But Jessica *hates* homework. Her favorite part of school is passing notes to her friends, so I thought she'd have fun writing to pen pals in Alaska. But Jessica drew Bob's name, and he's a boy. She thinks boys are gross. She calls Bob "Mooseboy" because he wears a big furry coat. I don't think that's very nice. She's never even met him!

"OK!" Mr. Crane clapped his hands.

"It's Winston's turn to be mailman."

Winston Egbert jumped up and plopped the blue mailman hat on his head. Then he reached into the bag and pulled out a letter.

"Ellen Riteman!" Winston read. He made a whooshing sound and tossed the letter like a Frisbee.

"No airmail delivery in class, please," Mr. Crane warned, grinning.

Winston started pretending he was driving a mail truck. "Mail for Todd Wilkins!" He handed Todd a letter. Then he zoomed up and down the rows of desks until the mailbag was empty.

Squeals and hoots of excitement filled the room as everyone tore open their mail.

"Look!" Lila cried. "Becky sent me

some earmuffs." They were pink and furry. Lila put them on.

"You look like an elephant," Winston said.

"A fat fuzzy one with floppy ears," Charlie Cashman added.

Lila stuck out her tongue.

"Hillary said the snow was over her head," Ellen announced.

I finished reading my letter. "Sally and her family had to ride the snowmobile to go to the store. Look, she sent a picture." I held it up for everyone to see. "The snowdrifts are taller than their house."

"Becky said they've been cross-country skiing." Lila tossed her head. "I've been cross-country skiing too, you know."

"Sam won the local sledding race," Winston said. "His dog's name is

Grizzly 'cause he looks like a bear."
Winston waved a photo of the big
black dog around.

"Oh, no," Jessica groaned as she
stared at her letter. Her face turned a
yucky green. "Oh, no, no, no!"

"What is it, Jess?" I asked, worried.
She looked like she wasn't feeling
well.

"This is awful," Jessica whispered.
She scrunched up her nose. I hoped
she wasn't going to be sick right there
in the room.

"Is it your letter? Let me see," I de-
manded.

Jessica hid her letter under her desk.
But I grabbed it and read it out loud.

Dear Jessica,
Guess what? I'm coming to
California! I'm going to stay with

my aunt. She says she'll bring me to your school. Then I can meet you and your twin sister and everyone in your class. See you soon!

Your pen pal,
Bob Burdett

"Wow!" I exclaimed. "Bob's coming to Sweet Valley!"

"We're going to meet a real boy from Alaska!" Jerry McAllister shouted. He gave Charlie a high five.

"I wonder if he'll bring us some raw fish," Winston said.

"I bet he'll be wearing that big furry moose coat," Andy Franklin added.

Everyone was smiling and talking. Everyone but Jessica. She still had that sick, green look on her face.

"Jess," I began, "this is *so* exciting. Everyone thinks so. Why aren't you happy?"

Jessica hunched over and moaned so loud that I ran and got the trash can.

CHAPTER 2

The Trouble with Boys

"Jessica, are you OK?" I asked.

"Mooseboy *can't* come to Sweet Valley Elementary!" Jessica whined. "He's a *boy*."

I shook my head. "Boys can be fun. Todd is."

"But Todd's not a furry, frozen, raw-fish-eating boy!" Jessica snapped.

"Oooh, Jessica's *boy*friend's coming to see her," Charlie teased.

Some of the other boys joined in. "Jessica's got a *boy*friend! Jessica's got a *boy*friend!"

Jessica covered her red cheeks with her hands. "See what I mean? Boys are *dumb!*"

"Don't pay attention to them," Eva Simpson whispered.

Mr. Crane gave the boys a warning look. They went back to sharing their letters.

I put my hand on Jessica's shoulder. "Just think, Jess. He can tell us what it's like to live in Alaska!"

"Maybe they have penguins there," Caroline Pearce added.

"I don't think so," I replied. "They have reindeer and caribou though. And seals and whales too. I saw it in a magazine."

"I don't care." Jessica sighed. "It was

10

bad enough just writing to him. But *meeting* him—*yuck!*"

"Why don't you like boys?" I asked.

"They're dumb," Jessica said. "And they sweat. And they burp out loud."

"Girls do too."

"Not as loud," Jessica insisted.

"Sandy Ferris does," Caroline said. "I heard her. She sounded just like one of the boys."

Ellen patted Jessica's hand in sympathy. "I'm glad he's not *my* pen pal. I wouldn't know what to do with him."

"Yeah!" Jessica cried, looking more worried than ever. "What will we do when he's here? It's not like I can play dress-up with him or anything."

"You can jump rope with him," I offered.

Jessica made a disgusted face. "Mooseboy won't know any of our rhymes. He probably doesn't know *anything* about normal stuff."

"What do you mean?" I asked. "He's from Alaska, not Mars."

"Yeah, but up there, they might not have cars and houses like us," Jessica argued. "They probably live in igloos."

"He can tell us all about that." I was getting more and more excited. "Maybe he'll bring pictures of what an igloo looks like on the inside. And he could tell us how they train the dogs to pull the sleds. It's going to be great."

Jessica looked at me like my head had just popped off. "It's going to be *awful!* I'll probably spend all my time explaining TV and stop signs and tacos and phones." Jessica threw up her hands. "You know, he might not even have electricity!"

"Then he can tell us how they stay warm without it in Alaska," I suggested. "Maybe he'll show us how to cook over a fire."

Jessica wrinkled her nose again. "If he doesn't have electricity, I bet it's too cold inside his igloo to take a bath."

"P.U.!" Ellen and Caroline said at the same time.

"Don't be mean, Jessica." I shook my head in disappointment. "I'm sure Bob takes baths."

Jessica pinched her nose. "What if he smells like a moose?"

Ellen and Caroline giggled. "Or a bear," Ellen said.

"Or fish. Yuck!" Caroline added.

Julie Porter and Eva began giggling.

"And don't forget," Jessica began, "boys spit too."

"Gross!" Julie covered her eyes.

"You aren't being fair, Jess," I complained. "You haven't even met Bob, and—"

"I have an idea," Jessica said. She snapped her fingers. "I'll make a list. I'll get some of the boys to help him." Jessica drew a picture of a face, then drew long squiggly lines like fur all around it. She wrote "Mooseboy" above it.

I gritted my teeth to keep from yelling at her. She was being so rude!

"Jerry can show him the playground." Jessica drew little boxes to make a chart. "And Charlie can teach him about electricity."

"I can't believe you're doing this," I

said. "*You* should be the one to show him things. *You're* his pen pal."

"And Winston can sit by him at lunch, since he likes to eat gross things anyway."

I bit my lip. I was really disappointed in Jessica. She should have been thinking of ways to make Bob feel welcome when he came to visit. Instead she was just being selfish and mean.

What if Jessica ruined his trip? Then Bob would go back and tell his classmates in Alaska about it. They would think all the kids at Sweet Valley were icky and awful. They'd probably stop writing to us. Even worse, they'd probably put a story in their newspaper: Kalifornia Kids Are Kreeps!

I made myself a promise. If Jessica wasn't going to treat Bob nicely, then I would. I couldn't let him go back to Alaska and say bad things about Sweet Valley Elementary!

CHAPTER 3

Home Sweet Alaska

"Mr. Crane?" I asked, carefully approaching his desk.

"Yes, Elizabeth?"

"I have an idea. . . ," I began, turning to look over my shoulder.

Jessica was still making her chart. She had just asked Ricky Capaldo to teach Bob how to eat with silverware.

I fidgeted in place. "Well . . . since there's so much snow in Alaska, could we decorate the room with snowflakes for Bob?"

Jessica stopped writing and glared at me.

"That would be fun!" Amy exclaimed.

"We could have a winter party here in California," Todd added.

"We could paint snow pictures," Julie suggested.

"Great idea." Mr. Crane seemed excited. "It'll fit in with our weather unit."

"We can eat ice cream," Winston said with a laugh. "Get it—ice, cold—you know—the *weather?*"

Some kids laughed, but most of the class made confused faces. Winston had a big problem when it came to making sense.

"When is Bob coming, Jessica?" Mr. Crane asked.

"On Friday," Jessica whispered.

I counted on my fingers. "That's only two days away."

"I bet I'll be sick that day," Jessica mumbled.

"We'll take care of decorations first thing Friday morning," Mr. Crane said. "But right now, we have to take care of science."

I frowned. I couldn't help but feel down with Jessica acting so grumpy.

The next day, Thursday, dragged. Jessica kept pouting about Bob and working on her list. On Friday, I couldn't wait to get to school. Jessica complained about being sick, but Mom could tell she was faking it and got her out of bed.

When we got to class, Mr. Crane already had the art supplies ready to make decorations. It looked like it was going to be fun.

"I've set up different centers around the room," Mr. Crane explained. "You can make paper snowflakes, paint snowy day pictures, make igloos out of sugar cubes, or make snowmen out of Styrofoam balls."

Lila skipped into the classroom looking proud. She was wearing a pink snowsuit with fluffy, furry trim. "Look what my mom sent me," she bragged, twirling around. "It's really expensive. It's from Switzerland."

"Pretty!" Ellen raced over to touch the fancy trim.

"I love it," Jessica said.

Charlie ran into the room. "Look what I brought." He held up a plastic bag with a huge chunk of ice in it.

"What is it?" Kisho Murasaki asked.

"It's a snowball. I made it by scraping the frost off the kitchen freezer."

"Cool," Jim Sturbridge said.

"I'm going to try that when I get home," Winston added.

"We could all make them and have a snowball fight," Jerry said.

"Wait a minute." Mr. Crane held up his hand in warning. "That snowball is solid ice. It would hurt someone if you hit them with it."

"I won't throw it," Charlie explained. "It's a present for Mooseboy."

"That's a . . . nice gesture, Charlie," Mr. Crane said, sounding confused. "Anyway, class, Bob's aunt called and said he'll be here in a couple of hours. So let's get to work on those decorations!"

Everyone scrambled to different parts of the room. I went to the snowflake-making table. Amy, Eva, and Lois Waller worked with me. We folded the paper into squares, then folded it again and again.

"You just cut in different places." Eva turned her square from side to side and snipped at the edges.

We all clipped and snipped away.

Tiny pieces of paper fluttered to the floor like little snowflakes. When I unfolded the big sheet of paper, I had a beautiful snowflake cutout. Soon we had a table full of them.

Lois pointed to our decorations. "All our snowflakes are different. None of them look the same."

"Neither do real snowflakes," Mr. Crane replied. "That's because no two snowflakes are alike."

"You mean there aren't any twin snowflakes?" I asked.

Mr. Crane laughed. "Nope!"

I looked over at Jessica, but she wasn't even helping with the decorations. She was still making her dumb list and walking from boy to boy.

"Would you show Mooseboy how to swing on a swing set?" she asked Todd.

"Would you take Mooseboy to the Sip-n-Munch?" she asked Ken Matthews.

"Would you show Mooseboy how a microwave works?" she asked Tom McKay.

Everyone she asked answered, "Yes!" They all seemed excited about doing something with Bob. And Jessica seemed excited to be getting rid of him.

I scowled. What if her plans backfired? She could really hurt Bob's feelings.

"Look at my painting." Sandy had painted a snowy scene with the sunshine trying to peek through.

"I made a snowman family." Amy held up her picture.

"And I painted an airplane flying through the snow," Winston said.

"It looks more like a bird," Charlie

said. "And it's crashing into the snow, not flying through it."

Winston flapped his arms like bird's wings. Then he "flew" into the wall and bonked his head.

I worry about Winston sometimes.

"I painted all kinds of bears in the snow," Kisho said holding up his painting. "Polar bears, grizzlies, brown bears, and baby bears."

"Wow!" I exclaimed. "The bears are so realistic."

"Look, everybody," Charlie shouted. "I drew a picture of Mooseboy and Jessica." In Charlie's drawing, Bob was covered in fur and had big antlers on his head. He was holding hands with Jessica. Big red hearts were drawn everywhere.

"Give me that!" Jessica said angrily. She snatched the drawing away from Charlie, wadded it up, and threw it in the trash.

Caroline, Jim, and Andy built igloos out of sugar cubes. They stuck the cubes together with white icing. Tom and Ken made snowmen out of Styrofoam balls and sat them on the table. They used pins to stick on raisins for eyes and used Chee-tos for noses. Then Mr. Crane helped Amy, Eva, Lois, and me hang the paper snowflakes.

"Hey, look." Jerry pointed out the window. Todd was sprinkling soap flakes in the trees. It looked exactly like snow falling on the branches!

"Guess what I did?" Winston whispered.

"What?" I asked.

"I turned up the air conditioner so it'd be cold in here."

"Why did you do that?" I rubbed my arms as cold air swirled around the room.

"Mooseboy lives where it's cold. Mr. Crane said some people have trouble getting used to different weather."

"You're right," I agreed. We didn't want Bob to get sick from the California heat!

The intercom interrupted our chatter. "Mr. Crane," the secretary's voice rang over the loudspeaker. "Bob Burdett is here."

"Great!" Mr. Crane said. "Would you bring him down, please? Thanks!"

"This is it!" I squealed.

"I can't believe it," Amy said.

"A real Alaskan!" Ellen clapped her hands in excitement.

"Another boy in the class!" Charlie pumped his fist in the air.

I glanced at Jessica. I hoped she would at least be smiling. But she was hiding behind Lila, who wouldn't take off her expensive pink snowsuit.

"I wonder if he'll have that big furry coat on," Lila whispered to Jessica.

Jessica made a sour face. "I hope not," she griped. "I'm embarrassed enough already!"

When Bob walked in, we gasped in surprise. We couldn't believe what he was wearing!

CHAPTER 4

Mooseboy's Surprise

"Hi, Bob," Mr. Crane said. "Welcome to Sweet Valley Elementary."

"Hi." Bob smiled and waved. He had dark wavy hair and big brown eyes. And he was wearing what any other boy in California would be wearing: a baseball T-shirt and jeans.

"He's not wearing his moose coat," I heard Ellen whisper to Jessica.

"Of course not," Eva

said. "It's too warm for a big furry coat."

"Mooseboy doesn't look weird to me," Julie commented. "He looks pretty normal."

"He's kind of cute," Amy whispered.

"He is!" Lila added quietly.

"Boys and girls, say hello to Bob," Mr. Crane said. "He's come a long way to visit us."

"Hi, Bob!" we chorused. I heard a few of the boys begin saying Mooseboy, but they stopped at the Moo.

Bob grinned. He was missing one of his bottom teeth.

"I'm Elizabeth Wakefield, Jessica's sister," I said quickly. I wanted to be sure that *someone* was polite to Bob.

"Hello," Bob said. "Nice to meet you."

I dragged Jessica out from behind Lila. "And this is your pen pal, Jessica."

"Hi," Jessica squeaked.

Bob shifted from foot to foot. "Hi, Jessica," he said quietly, looking back and forth at each of us. "You two sure do look alike. Even more than in your school pictures."

"You can tell them apart by their name bracelets," Ellen explained. She picked up Jessica's arm and pointed to it.

"I'll have to remember that," Bob replied.

We took turns telling Bob our names. Bob seemed dizzy from trying to remember all of them. He looked the way I always felt after taking a timed test.

"Tell us about your trip," Mr. Crane said.

"Well, I got here yesterday. I'm visiting my aunt."

"Do you live in an igloo?" Winston asked.

Bob laughed and shook his head. "I live in a house."

"What's it made out of? Mud?" Jim asked.

"Mine's made of logs."

"Do you have TVs and stuff in Alaska?" Jerry asked.

"Yeah . . . we've pretty much got the same stuff as you have," Bob replied.

"Except we don't have all that snow!" I added.

"Right," Bob said with a smile. "We have tons of it."

"Do you have cars in Alaska?" Charlie asked.

Bob smiled. "Sure. Sometimes the roads get so thick with snow we can't use them. But the snowplows come around every morning."

"Isn't it freezing?" Eva asked, shivering.

"It gets pretty cold," Bob replied.

"How cold?" I asked.

"Sometimes below zero. And we don't see the sun much. Part of the time we go to school in the dark and come home in the dark." Bob rubbed his hands up and down his arms. "But we bundle up and wear hats and stuff to keep warm."

"Do you really go snowmobiling and use dogsleds?" Charlie asked.

Bob nodded. "Sometimes we skate on the pond. Or we ski at recess."

"That sounds cool!" Charlie acted like he was skiing. "Man, I want to go to school in Alaska."

Bob smiled. "But we don't have swimming pools in our backyards like you do here."

"You *don't?*" Lila looked shocked. "That's *awful!*"

Bob shook his head. "We wouldn't use an outdoor pool much. It doesn't really get hot enough outside."

"Look, Bob! We decorated the room for you." Eva swept her arm around the classroom. "We even made snowmen."

"We made paper snowflakes too." I pointed to the ceiling where the snowflakes dangled.

"Awesome." Bob glanced around the room. "What's the white stuff in the trees outside?"

"That's supposed to be snow," Todd told him. "But it's really soap."

"Hey, Bob, I made you a snowball from my freezer." Charlie picked up the plastic bag, but part of the snowball had melted. When he handed it to Bob, water dribbled out of the bag and all over Bob's hand.

"Wow! That's cold!" Bob exclaimed,

laughing as he wiped his hand on his jeans.

"I thought you'd be used to it." Charlie looked confused.

"Cold is cold, no matter what," Bob replied, chuckling. "Even if you live in freezing weather all year round, you still get cold."

"We made sugar cube igloos," Jerry pointed out. "They're not made out of ice, so you won't get frozen."

Bob looked impressed. "Could I take one of those home?" he asked. "We've never made anything like that at our school."

"Sure," Mr. Crane said. "We'd be honored."

"Oh, I almost forgot." Bob took his book bag off his back. "I brought some things for the class." He dug inside and pulled out a small flag. "This is our state flag. It's blue with gold stars like the Big Dipper." Then he took out a carving of a dog. "My dad carves figures from wood. He helped me make it."

"Awesome!" the boys said. Even the girls looked interested.

"And these are snowshoes." He held up a pair of tiny wooden snowshoes tied with ribbon. "You're supposed to hang them over your door for good luck."

"Can we hang them up, Mr. Crane?" I asked.

"Sure." Mr. Crane hung them over the doorway so that every time we passed through, we could see them.

"I knew Bob would be cool," I whispered to Jessica.

Jessica silently fidgeted with her hands.

"What else do you have in there?" Lila asked.

Bob's face turned red. "Nothing much." He quickly zipped the bag.

My eyes narrowed. Was he hiding something?

CHAPTER 5

Making a List, Checking It Twice . . .

"OK, everyone, It's time for recess," Mr. Crane announced. "Jessica, since you're Bob's pen pal, you can show him around the playground."

Jessica froze and yanked at my hand. Her cheeks turned as red as tomatoes.

"Go on, Jess," I whispered.

"Uh . . . , " Jessica stammered. "I . . . I made this list. That way . . . that way everyone can play with Bob." She ran to her desk and pulled out her list. "OK. Jerry's supposed to take you to the playground."

Bob gave Jessica a strange look and shrugged. "All right."

"Come on," Jerry said. "We've got a great playground."

While Bob and Jerry talked, everyone lined up. I tried to talk to Jessica, but she ignored me and scooted next to Lila. Lila's face was turning a little red. I guessed it was because she was hot in her snowsuit.

As soon as we reached the playground, Jessica ran off with Lila to jump rope. Bob followed Jerry to the monkey bars and they climbed up.

Winston climbed behind them. "Eeek! Eeek! Eeek!" he screeched as he swung his arms and acted like an ape.

"Let's play soccer." Todd got the soccer ball and kicked it around.

"Great." I waved to Bob and Jerry. "You guys want to play?"

"Sure!" Bob hopped down and ran over.

We divided into teams. Jerry, Bob, and Todd played against Eva, Amy, and me.

"Do you play soccer at your school?" Todd asked Bob.

"Sometimes. Mostly we play ice hockey or just skate."

"On the lake?" Charlie asked.

"Yeah, it freezes to solid ice," Bob said.

"I'd like to do that," I said.

"You'd be good at it, Liz." Todd kicked the ball and I stopped it with my foot.

I grinned and passed it to Amy. For the next few minutes we dribbled and passed and had a great time.

"Uh-oh, time to go

in," Jerry said when Mrs. Grimley, the recess monitor, blew her whistle.

After recess, we hurried to lunch. Jessica pulled her list from her pocket. "Winston, you can sit next to Bob."

Bob took a tray and sat down. Winston opened his sack and wolfed down his peanut butter and mayonnaise sandwich. Jessica sat all the way at the other end of the table. She was really making me mad.

"This food looks pretty good," Bob said, picking up his piece of pizza.

"What's your favorite food?" I asked.

"Fish?" Charlie asked.

"Moose?" Jerry added.

Todd put down his fork. "Bear meat?"

Bob chuckled. "Pizza."

Everyone laughed.

Bob picked off a piece of pepperoni. "But my favorite pizza has pineapple on it."

"That's funny," I said. "That's Jessica's favorite too."

"Really?" Bob asked. "Wow, I thought I was the only kid who liked pineapple pizza."

I looked over to where Jessica was sitting, hoping she had overheard. But she was obviously trying to ignore us.

"Jessica, why aren't you being nicer to Bob?" I whispered as we lined up to walk back to the room.

She shrugged. "He's having fun with the boys. He doesn't even notice."

I scowled. I didn't think that was true. I wanted to tell Jessica about how Bob liked pineapple pizza, but she was too busy going over her list.

CHAPTER 6
A Cold Return

When we filed into the classroom, it felt like a big freezer. The cold air made goose bumps shimmy up my arms. Jessica shivered. My teeth chattered. It was so cold I expected to see icicles hanging off the window panes.

"I'm cold," Amy whispered.

"Me too," Eva agreed. She rubbed her arms and jumped up and down to warm herself. Everyone else bounced up and down too, except Lila, who looked happy in her snowsuit.

"It's freezing in here." Bob rubbed his

hands together. "I thought California was supposed to be warm."

Mr. Crane looked at the thermostat. "Someone turned the air conditioning on high. No wonder it's so cold in here." He switched the dial to low.

"It wasn't me," Winston insisted, wrapping his arms around himself.

"I need a sweater," Eva said. "I'm . . . sha-shaking."

"Well *I'm* not cold." Lila showed off, brushing the fur on her snowsuit.

Jim groaned. "Maybe not. But you look like a pink snowball."

"Or a big puff of cotton candy," Charlie added.

Mr. Crane searched the lost and found box.

"Here, everyone find something warm."

I grabbed a blue jacket. Jessica found a pink sweater. Winston put on a green, polka-dotted girls' sweater.

"You look like you're in the circus," Jerry said.

Charlie found a faded denim jacket, and Jerry pulled on a big long shirt that fell to his knees.

"That looks like a dress," Ricky teased, putting on the last sweater. It was a long, orange fuzzy one.

"At least I don't look like a pumpkin," Charlie said. "Ricky, Ricky, pumpkin icky."

Mr. Crane gave Charlie a warning look.

"A pumpkin's better than a moose," Jessica whispered to me.

"Jessica, that's mean," I said. But Jessica just went back to checking her list.

"OK, class." Mr. Crane clapped his hands together. "Let's get back to science for a moment. When we're talking about weather, we're talking about liquids, solids, and gases. Now we're going to freeze water, melt ice cubes, and watch water evaporate."

He placed a hot plate on the science table and turned it on. "This gets really hot, so please be careful and don't touch it. OK . . . Jessica, Todd, and Ricky, please fill those plastic containers with water." They did as he said. "Jerry, Sandy, please take them to the cafeteria and ask the lunchroom workers to put them in the freezer for us." Then Mr. Crane placed a pot of water on one side of the hot plate. "We'll heat this water and watch it evaporate."

"That's steam, right?" Bob asked.

"Very good, Bob," Mr. Crane said.

"Now we're going to place ice cubes in the other pot and watch them melt."

We all gathered around the science table. The hot plate burners turned bright orange. Soon small bubbles popped up in the water. Then steam swirled above the pot.

"It's evaporating," Mr. Crane said.

"It's getting warm in here too," Ellen said. She took off her sweater.

"Yeah, it's getting hot." Charlie took off his jacket. Ricky pulled off the pumpkin sweater and tossed it in the box.

"So . . . hot . . . ," Lila squeaked.

"Lila, are you all right?" Jessica asked.

Lila leaned against the table. Her cheeks were rosy and sweat dribbled down her cheek.

"It's that big pink fur ball she's wearing," Charlie said.

"Lila, do you have something else to change into?" Mr. Crane asked.

Lila nodded sadly. She was probably upset that she couldn't show off anymore.

"I'll go with her," Jessica offered. The two of them left for the girls' bathroom. When they came back, Lila still looked flushed.

"See, all the ice has melted." Mr. Crane gave us each a turn to look into the pot. There was only water inside.

"Lila almost melted too," Jerry said.

"Yeah," Charlie hissed. "Like the Wicked Witch of the West!"

I frowned. It wasn't nice of Charlie to say that, but then again, I'd been thinking bad things about Lila too. Maybe the way Jessica was being mean to Bob was catching, like a nasty cold.

After the experiment was over, Bob's aunt came to pick him up. She looked just like any other aunt. We all waved good-bye.

Bob looked at my sister. "Good-bye, Jessica," he said.

"Bye," she answered quietly.

Jerry and Charlie covered their mouths and made kissy faces behind their hands. I gave them a look and they stopped.

Bob didn't seem to have noticed. He waved to everybody and said, "See you tomorrow, Lila," just before he and his aunt left the room.

"Tomorrow?" Winston asked. "But tomorrow's Saturday."

Jessica's face scrunched up. "Yeah, Lila. What are you up to?"

Jerry and Charlie made more kissy faces and chuckled.

Lila smiled slyly. "I'm having a party tomorrow at Fowler Crest. And you're all invited!"

Everyone cheered.

"It's a surprise snow party for Moose—I mean, Bob," Lila continued. "My daddy is renting a snowmaking machine so Bob can feel at home."

A party with real snow! It was a fantastic idea.

But Jessica obviously didn't feel the same. She looked down at the floor and pushed a scrap of paper around with the toe of her sneaker. I knew she wouldn't miss her best friend's party. But I just hoped she wouldn't ignore Bob like she did today.

CHAPTER 7

Snow Fun

"Let's wear our matching sweatshirts with the snowflakes on them," Jessica said on Saturday morning. She was beginning to act excited about the snow party at Lila's house. I wondered if she was just pretending.

"OK. And we'll wear the new parkas Grandma sent us."

"Hey, goofballs. What are you doing wearing sweatshirts and jackets?" Steven asked when we ran downstairs. "You've even got hats and mittens too. It's warm outside, weirdos."

"Lila's having a snow party," I said. "Her dad hired a snow machine and everything!"

"Is this a party for your *boy*friend, Jessica?" Steven teased.

Jessica frowned. "Mooseboy's *not* my boyfriend."

"Bob is really nice," I said. "He says they ice skate during recess on the frozen pond by their school."

"Wow!" Steven seemed impressed. "Too bad you can't go visit him there . . . and never come back."

Jessica poked his arm. "Very funny."

Mom hurried in. "Are you ready, girls? Let's head over to Fowler Crest."

Jessica and I ran to the car.

When we got there, we both gasped at how beautiful Fowler Crest looked. Two men in hats and jumpsuits were working the snowmaking machine in

Lila's huge backyard. Cold air and icy powder whirled out of the machine. The whole yard looked like it was covered with a soft white blanket. Most of the kids from the class were already there playing.

"Have fun, girls," Mom said as we climbed out of the car.

"We will!" Jessica and I cheered at the same time. As soon as I jumped out, I grabbed a handful of the snow and tossed it at Jessica. White flakes dotted her hat and face.

"Eeek!" she squealed. She bent

down, scooped up some snow, and threw it at me.

Lila came running over in her pink snowsuit. "Isn't this amazing?"

"It's so pretty!" Jessica cried.

"I never thought we'd get snow like this in California!" I added. "This is going to be a great party."

"Thanks." Lila grinned happily.

"Is Bob here yet?" I asked.

"No," Lila answered. "He'll be here a little later. He's going to be so surprised!"

I snuck a look at Jessica. She looked relieved. Maybe she was hoping that Bob wouldn't show up at all.

"Come on," Lila said as Eva, Ellen, Amy, and Todd came over. "We've got hot chocolate."

"She has a snow cone machine and a cake in the shape of a snowman too," Ellen said.

We went to the picnic tables and drank hot chocolate and ate snow cones. I took a drink of hot chocolate and then bit into a snow cone. It felt so cold, I thought my teeth were going to break!

Winston took a gulp of hot chocolate and waved his hand in front of his mouth like it was burning. He plopped some of his lime snow cone in his mug to cool it down. When he drank some more, he made a face and poured it out under the picnic table when Lila wasn't looking.

"When are we going to have some cake?" Caroline asked.

"After Bob gets here," Lila replied. She took Jessica's hand. "Come on, let's go play."

"OK!" Jessica said. The two of them ran toward a big snow pile that had some sleds lined up next to it.

Everyone took off in little groups and played in the snow. Caroline and Ellen turned cartwheels and tumbled. Lois and Kisho started piling snow to make a snowman.

Todd took a soccer ball out of his duffel bag. "Let's play snow soccer, Elizabeth."

"Great!" We went out and kicked the ball around in the snow. The snow made it hard to run fast, and before long we were huffing and puffing.

"Hey, everybody!" I heard someone shout. "What's going on? Where did all this snow come from?"

I turned around and saw Bob standing at the entrance to the Fowlers' backyard with his aunt. He was wearing jeans and a T-shirt, and his eyes were wide.

"Hi, Bob!" we chorused. "Surprise!"

Lila came running over as Bob's aunt said good-bye. Jessica lagged behind her. *Way* behind.

Bob still looked shocked. "Snow in California?"

"We're having a snow party for you!" Eva said.

"It was Lila's idea," I added, keeping an eye on Jessica. She was standing in the back by a palm tree. "Her dad got the snowmaking machine."

Bob smiled at me. "Hi, Jessica. I didn't recognize you. You're all bundled up."

I giggled. "I'm actually Elizabeth. Jessica is over . . . there," I pointed out, hoping Jessica would be nice and say hi.

"Hi, Jessica!" Bob repeated, waving to her.

Jessica gave a little wave but didn't say anything back.

Bob brushed some snow from his hair. "I can't believe all this snow. It's so weird."

"I know, isn't it *cool?*" Lila said, grinning.

Bob laughed a little. I was surprised that he didn't seem more excited about the snow. Was something wrong?

Was he mad at my sister?

I gulped. I hoped not! If he was, the party would be a disaster!

CHAPTER 8

Pen Pal Problems

Bob rubbed his bare arms. "I'm a little cold. Does anyone have a sweater or something I can borrow?"

"Here." Todd took off his parka, hat, and mittens. "I've got lots of warm clothes on, so I don't need these as much as you do."

"Thanks, Todd."

One of the Fowlers' butlers appeared. "Lunch is served," he announced.

We all sat at the picnic tables while we were served lunch. I'd never seen so many hot dogs in one place before!

"I thought that hot dogs would be the perfect snow-day food," Lila said. "Have you ever had a hot dog, Bob?"

"Of course," he said.

After lunch we drank hot chocolate and ate cake. Everyone was chatting and talking—everyone but Bob and Jessica. They were both really quiet.

"Mmm, this cake is really good," I said, turning to Bob. "Isn't it good, Bob?"

Bob shrugged. "Yeah, the cake's good."

As soon as we were finished, we ran out to play in the snow.

Lila flopped down on her back. "Here's how to make a snow angel," she said. "I learned how on a ski trip." She waved her arms and swept her legs back and forth. When she got up, there was an angel shape in the snow.

Winston quickly copied Lila. "Look, I'm a snow angel!"

"No, you're a snow *clown*." Charlie laughed.

We all joined in. Even Jessica. But not Bob. He just sat and watched us.

"Don't you want to make one, Bob?" Todd asked.

"Nah. I'm kind of tired." Bob picked up a stick and scribbled designs in the snow.

Jerry, Charlie, Ricky, and Jim ran to the big snow hill and went sledding. Lois and Kisho went back to building their snow-man. Winston began making *himself* into a snowman by kneeling down and piling snow around his legs.

Lila brought out

a box of plastic bags. "Here, put these bags on your feet," she said. "We can pretend we're ice skating."

Ellen, Amy, Todd, and I slipped on the bags and slid across the yard.

"This is fun!" I shouted.

"Come on, Bob," Lila said. "Don't you want to try it?"

Bob sipped a cup of hot chocolate and shook his head. "No, thanks. I think I'll skip it."

I slid and fell on my bottom. Amy and Todd laughed. Then I noticed Jessica sitting by herself in the snow. She looked sad. So did Bob.

Was Jessica feeling bad about the way she'd treated Bob?

Had she done something really mean to him?

I brushed off the seat of my pants and skated over to Jessica. I sat down beside her. "What's wrong, Jess?"

Jessica bit her bottom lip and shrugged.

"It's a great party," I said.

"Yeah," Jessica replied in a low voice.

"Bob looks upset," I said. "Did you say something to him?"

"No." Jessica's bottom lip quivered. "I know I haven't been very nice to him. But I didn't want everyone teasing me and saying he's my boyfriend and stuff."

"Who cares about that?" I said. "Bob's really nice, Jess. You should be more friendly."

"I know." Jessica blushed.

"So . . . you like Bob?"

"Well, yeah. I mean . . . " Jessica looked around as if she didn't want anyone to hear. "Um, he's not bad for a boy."

I put my arm around her. "It's not too late to tell him you're sorry."

Jessica patted the snow. "I guess you're right. But what if he doesn't want to talk to me?"

"I bet he will."

Jessica pouted. "But what do I say?"

"Just say you're sorry. Then ask him to play."

We watched Bob for a minute. He stared at the ground and dragged the toe of his sneaker in the snow. It looked exactly like what Jessica was doing yesterday after Bob left class. Then I remembered something else they had in common!

"Hey, Jess," I began. "Why not talk to him about pineapple pizza?"

Jessica raised her eyebrows. "Why?"

"That's Bob's favorite kind of pizza too."

"Really!" She smiled. "Wow. Um . . . OK. I'll do it."

Jessica stood up and nervously headed

toward Bob. She almost turned around at one point, but then she hurried over to Bob and began talking.

I tried to listen in, but stopped. It wasn't nice to snoop. But before long I saw that they were both smiling and talking. What a relief!

Suddenly I saw Lila run over with a snowball. She threw it at Jessica. It hit Jessica's hat. She looked like she had vanilla frosting on her head.

I got up and dashed over. Was Lila jealous? Was she trying to mess things up?

When I got there, I heard everyone giggling. Thank goodness! Lila wasn't trying to be mean at all. She was just playing.

"I'll get you back," Jessica said, smiling. "Come on, Bob. Let's cream her!" She made her own snowball and pitched it toward Lila. Lila screamed and threw one back. Then Jessica and

Bob ganged up on me and Lila. Snowballs were flying everywhere!

Soon all the kids joined in. The snowball fight was so huge that I hadn't even noticed that Bob wasn't there anymore.

I looked around for him. He was swinging by himself on the swing set, watching us. Winston came over and dumped a huge bucket of snow over my head, but I couldn't laugh. Bob just seemed so sad. Was all the snow making him homesick?

CHAPTER 9

Sunshine Please!

On Monday at school, Bob joined us again. Everyone talked and laughed about the party.

"Mr. Crane, you should have been there," I said. "The party was great."

"It sounds like fun," Mr. Crane said. "Lila's father was really nice to do all that."

Everyone kept chattering in excited voices, but Bob just stared out the window. He still looked sad. Maybe he was bored. Maybe he didn't like California and would go back and tell everyone in Alaska that Sweet Valley Elementary was no fun.

That didn't make any sense. The party had been a lot of fun. And Bob had a good time playing soccer with us at recess on Friday. Jessica was being nice to him too. What was wrong?

"Let's start the day by talking about the weather," Mr. Crane said. "What is snow?"

"Frozen rain," Charlie yelled.

"Ice," Ellen suggested.

"You're both right," Mr. Crane said. "Snow is formed when moisture from the clouds hits the air. The weather conditions have to be just right."

"It never snows here because it doesn't

get cold enough," Amy said. "Right, Mr. Crane?"

"Yes . . . and no," Mr. Crane replied. "It rarely snows in southern California. But every once in a while, when the conditions are just right, it does."

"I guess the conditions are right all the time in Alaska, aren't they?" I asked Bob.

Bob nodded gloomily.

"What's wrong, Bob?" I asked gently. "I know pretend snow isn't as much fun as the real thing—"

"It's not that," Bob insisted. "The party was great."

"Then what's the matter?" I continued. "Are you homesick?"

Bob shrugged and pointed outside. "I guess I was looking forward to some real California sunshine. I'm sick of snow."

Lila gasped. I felt the corners of my mouth droop.

"And we gave you more snow," I said. "Just what you didn't want."

"Oh, no," the class groaned.

Jessica leaned over and poked my arm. "I know what we could do," she whispered.

"What?"

"Mr. Crane could take Bob and us on a field trip to the beach."

I brightened up. "You're a genius!" I whispered.

"What?" Mr. Crane asked.

"Let's take a field trip to the beach," Jessica and I blurted out at the same time.

Bob grinned. "You mean it?"

Mr. Crane looked thoughtful for a

moment. "That sounds like a good idea."

"When can we go?" Jerry asked.

Mr. Crane scratched his chin. "How about this Friday? It's Bob's last day with us."

Everyone cheered.

"Thanks." Bob's smile was so big it almost swallowed his face. He stood up, rushed over, and hugged Jessica. "You're the best pen pal ever, Jessica," he said.

I expected Jessica to gag. But Jessica beamed instead. I guess she decided boys weren't so gross after all!

CHAPTER 10
Sweet Valley Blizzard!

"I thought Friday would never get here," I said when we boarded the bus for the field trip.

"Me neither." Bob sat down beside Winston, and Jessica and I sat behind them. Bob looked really ready for the beach, with his bright sunglasses, his wild swimming trunks, and his pale skin. He even brought a shark beach towel.

"Hope you have lots of sunscreen," Charlie warned.

"I do." Winston popped up over the

seat with a neon green nose. "This stuff does the trick."

"You won't get sunburned and you'll scare away the sharks at the same time," Jerry joked.

"Are there really sharks?" Bob asked.

"Not where we're going," Mr. Crane said. "It's safe. Just remember to stay close to the parent chaperones."

When we pulled up and unloaded at the beach, Bob jumped up and down. "This is awesome!"

I smiled. "There's no snow in sight. Just lots of sand and water for you."

"I can't wait to tell everyone back home about it." Bob raised his face toward the sky. "The sun feels so warm."

"Let's chase the waves," Jessica said.

We ran along the ocean's edge, dashing back and forth as the water rushed in and out.

"You're pretty fast, Jessica," Bob told her.

Jessica's cheeks turned red. "Thanks, Bob."

I smiled. Jessica wasn't calling Bob "Mooseboy" anymore!

We played until everyone got tired and thirsty. Then the parents gave us juice boxes.

"Look, there's a surfer!" Bob pointed out toward the ocean.

"Surfing is really hard," Jessica said.

Bob looked surprised. "You know how to surf?"

Jessica giggled. "No. But I tried to stand on my float once and fell off."

"I wish we could try it,"

Bob said. "It'd be fun to go in the water."

"The water's too cold today." I stuck my big toe in and shivered.

"Hey, Bob, you want to catch some raw fish and eat it?" Ricky asked. He lowered a net into the water and scooped it up.

Bob made a face. "Actually, I don't like raw fish. I can't believe you guys eat it."

Jessica and I traded confused looks.

"What do you mean?" Jessica asked. "We don't eat raw fish. We thought *you* did."

"Yeah," Charlie said. "Don't people in Alaska eat all kinds of weird stuff?"

Bob shook his head. "No way. I heard that you all ate sushi in California. I was afraid you were going to make me eat it too." He shivered.

"I'd never eat raw fish. That's gross."

Everyone burst into laughter.

"We had some pretty crazy ideas about each other, I guess," I said.

"Time for hamburgers," Mrs. Riteman, one of the chaperones, called.

We ran over to the grills and sat down on the picnic blankets the chaperones had laid out.

"Now *this* is what I thought California was all about," Bob said before he bit into his hamburger.

Jessica smiled. "I guess we're so used to doing stuff like this that we don't even think about it."

After a while the sun slipped behind a cloud and it turned chilly. I rubbed my hands up and down my arms. Some of the guys started playing tag. It looked like a good way to keep warm.

"Let's play in the sand," I suggested.

We played tag for a while and then started building things out of sand. Ricky, Bob, and Charlie built a sand shark. Jessica, Ellen, Amy, and I built a huge castle. Winston made a moat around it and filled it with water.

As we worked, the sun faded. The sky grew darker and darker. A soft breeze flitted through the air.

"It looks like it's going to rain," Jessica said.

She was right. The air felt cold and damp. The wind blew harder. And the sky grew black with dark clouds. But it didn't rain.

It started snowing instead!

I was so excited my stomach jiggled. Tiny white snowflakes fluttered all around us. Then the flakes grew bigger.

"Look!" Jessica squealed. "It's sticking to the sand."

"Snow, snow!" the other kids yelled. "It's our first snow!"

"We're having a blizzard!" Winston yelled.

Everyone ran around, trying to catch the snowflakes. Winston stuck out his tongue and caught a snowflake on the tip.

"I guess I should have brought my big furry coat after all," Bob joked.

Jerry and Charlie laughed.

"You must have brought part of Alaska with you," Jessica said.

"I'm sorry, Bob," I apologized. "We didn't know it was going to snow today. Honest." I felt so bad for him. We were all excited to see the snow, but he was sick of it.

"It's OK," Bob insisted. "I got to see the beach and the ocean. And make a sand shark too."

"Here," Jessica said. She handed him a beautiful conch shell and a plastic bag filled with sand. "You can take part of California home with you."

"Thanks, Jessica." Bob dug his toe in the sand and stirred it around. "I . . . I have something for you too. My mom wanted me to give it to you."

"What?" Jessica asked.

Bob ran over and opened up his book bag. Jessica's eyes widened in surprise when Bob handed her a beautiful porcelain doll with long dark braids.

"It's a real Eskimo doll!" Jessica squealed.

Bob grinned, but he seemed a little embarrassed too. Jessica hugged the doll to her chest and brushed the snowflakes away as they fell into the doll's hair.

The doll was beautiful. So *that* was what he was hiding on Friday!

"Thanks," Jessica said, smiling at Bob. "I always wanted an Eskimo doll."

"Come on, you guys!" Lila yelled. "Let's play in the snow."

Jessica and I traded looks.

"Go ahead," Bob said. "You play in the snow. I'll play in the sand."

Jessica and I danced around and held out our hands as the snowflakes fell. Bob wrote our names in the sand with a stick. It was the best field trip ever—a beach trip for Bob and a Sweet Valley blizzard for us!

Mr. Crane's class is marching in a big St. Patrick's Day parade—and they're playing real musical instruments! Which twin will make the most noise? Find out in Sweet Valley Kids #75, LITTLE DRUMMER GIRLS.

Elizabeth's Cool Crossword

Elizabeth remembered ten things that happened in the story. But after she wrote them out, she erased a word or name from each sentence!

When you figure out what the missing word or name is, fill in the blanks. Then you can write the missing word in the matching crossword spaces!

Can you get all ten words right without peeking back at the story? Good luck!

ACROSS
1. Bob's last name is _____.
2. Lila got hot wearing her _____ in class.
3. The kids drank hot _____ at Lila's party.
4. Mr. Crane made _____ by heating a pan of water on a hot plate.
5. Amy and Lila thought Bob was _____.

DOWN
1. The state flag of Alaska is _____ with gold stars.
2. Lila's house is called Fowler _____.
3. Bob and Jessica both like _____ on their pizza.
4. Bob gave Jessica an _____ doll.
5. Some of the kids made igloos out of _____ cubes.

Jessica's Wacky Letter

Jessica wants to write a letter to her pen pal Bob, but she can't find the right words! You can help her by filling in the blanks. Just fill in each blank with a word that fits the part of speech written underneath it. For example:

Noun—*a person, place, or thing:* snow, sled, beach, pen pal, friend

Verb—*an action:* going, asking, singing, throwing, laughing

Adjective—*a word that describes a noun:* pretty, silly, boring, ugly, fun

If you ask a friend for the different words without showing her or him the letter, it could turn out really funny! Try it!

Dear Bob,

How are you? I hope your trip back to Alaska was _____. We all liked meeting
            adjective
you. It was really _____ when we went
                    adjective
to the _____.
        noun

What was your favorite California food? I thought it was really _____ when you
                                adjective
ate a _____. Did it taste _____?
        noun   adjective

Lila says hi. She thinks you're _____.
                                adjective
Isn't that _____?
            adjective

Tomorrow we're going to talk about _____
                                    noun
in class. You know I'll be _____!
                            verb

We miss you, Bob! Write back soon!

                        Your pen pal,
                        Jessica

Answer to Elizabeth's Cool Crossword

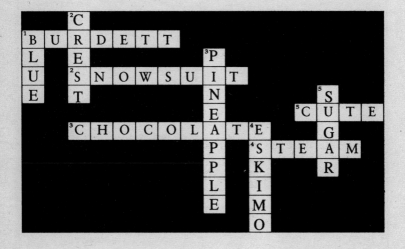

SIGN UP FOR THE SWEET VALLEY HIGH® FAN CLUB!

Hey, girls! Get all the gossip on Sweet Valley High's® most popular teenagers when you join our fantastic Fan Club! As a member, you'll get all of this really cool stuff:

- Membership Card with your own personal Fan Club ID number
- A Sweet Valley High® Secret Treasure Box
- Sweet Valley High® Stationery
- Official Fan Club Pencil (for secret note writing!)
- Three Bookmarks
- A "Members Only" Door Hanger
- Two Skeins of J. & P. Coats® Embroidery Floss with flower barrette instruction leaflet
- Two editions of *The Oracle* newsletter
- Plus exclusive Sweet Valley High® product offers, special savings, contests, and much more!

Be the first to find out what Jessica & Elizabeth Wakefield are up to by joining the Sweet Valley High® Fan Club for the one-year membership fee of only $6.25 each for U.S. residents, $8.25 for Canadian residents (U.S. currency). Includes shipping & handling.

Send a check or money order (do not send cash) made payable to "Sweet Valley High® Fan Club" along with this form to:

SWEET VALLEY HIGH® FAN CLUB, BOX 3919-B, SCHAUMBURG, IL 60168-3919

NAME_____
(Please print clearly)

ADDRESS_____

CITY_____ STATE _____ ZIP_____
(Required)

AGE_____ BIRTHDAY_____ /_____ /_____